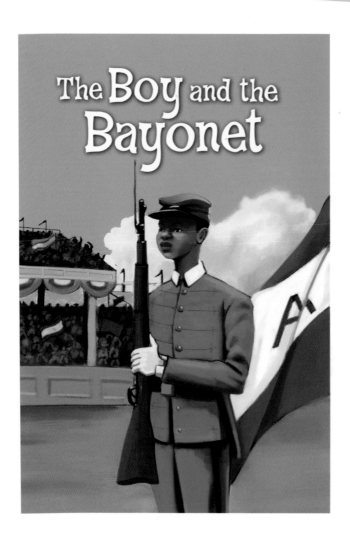

The Boy and the Bayonet

By Paul Laurence Dunbar
Illustrated by Luigi Savino

Publishing Credits

Rachelle Cracchiolo, M.S.Ed., *Publisher*
Conni Medina, M.A.Ed., *Editor in Chief*
Nika Fabienke, Ed.D., *Content Director*
Véronique Bos, *Creative Director*
Shaun N. Bernadou, *Art Director*
Seth Rogers, *Editor*
Valerie Morales, *Associate Editor*
Kevin Pham, *Graphic Designer*

Image Credits

Illustrated by Luigi Savino

Library of Congress Cataloging-in-Publication Data

Names: Dunbar, Paul Laurence, 1872-1906, author.
Title: The boy and the bayonet / by Paul Laurence Dunbar.
Description: Huntington Beach, CA : Teacher Created Materials, [2019] |
    Audience: Ages 13 | Audience: Grades 4-6 | Summary: Bud is inconsolable
    after making a mistake during the 1895 end-of-year Cadet Corps drill
    competition while his mother and Little Sister watch. Includes "Book
    Club Questions."
Identifiers: LCCN 2019026426 (print) | LCCN 2019026427 (ebook) | ISBN
    9781644913550 (paperback) | ISBN 9781644914458 (ebook)
Subjects: CYAC: Military cadets--Fiction. | Conduct of life--Fiction. |
    African Americans--Fiction. | Single-parent families--Fiction. | Family
    life--Washington (D.C.)--Fiction. | Washington (D.C.)--History--19th
    century--Fiction.
Classification: LCC PZ7.D89443 Boy 2019 (print) | LCC PZ7.D89443 (ebook)
    | DDC [Fic]--dc23
LC record available at https://lccn.loc.gov/2019026426
LC ebook record available at https://lccn.loc.gov/2019026427

5301 Oceanus Drive
Huntington Beach, CA 92649-1030
www.tcmpub.com

ISBN 978-1-6449-1355-0

Table of Contents

CHAPTER ONE

❈

Family Pride

It was June 1895, near the end of school. The air was full of the sound of the bustle and preparation for the final exercises, field day, and drills. Especially drills. Nothing so gladdens the heart of a Washington mother, be she black or white, as seeing her boy in a blue cadet's uniform, marching proudly to the cheers of the crowd.

The uniform had the power to make a boy forget the many nights when he had come in tired out and dusty from his practice drill. It lightened the memories of a mother carrying the weight of the home on her shoulders. She feels only the pride and joy of the result.

Bud did all he could to help the family outside of study hours. But there had been many days of hard work for Hannah Davis since her son started at the high school. And she did it gladly, since it gave Bud the chance to learn. It gave Bud a chance at things that had passed her by long ago.

When he entered the Cadet Corps, it seemed to be a first step toward the fulfillment of all her hopes. It was hard for her, getting the uniform. But Bud helped do his part. When his mother saw him rigged out in all his regimentals, she felt that it was worth all the trouble and expense just to see

the joy and pride of Little Sister, who adored Bud.

As the time for the drill competition drew near, there was an air of excitement in the little house on D Street, where the three lived. Too sickly for school, Little Sister sat all day long and looked out the window on the dull prospect of a dusty street lined on either side with dull red brick houses, all the same ugly pattern. Sprinkled here and there were older, uglier frame shanties. In the evening, Hannah hurried home to get supper ready before the time when Bud would return, hungry and tired from his drills and the chore work that followed them.

When Little Sister saw Bud, she was energized. Her questions about school followed him all through the house. When Little Sister looked at Bud, she saw her hero.

CHAPTER TWO

The Great Day

Things were cheerful. As they ate supper, Bud, with glowing face, would tell just how his Company A was doing, every move and every command. He would explain in great detail just what they were going to do to Companies B and C. It was not bragging so much as showing confidence based on the hard work he was doing.

Little Sister often, listening to her brother, would clap her hands or cry, "Oh, Bud, you're just splendid an' I know you'll beat 'em!"

"If we work hard, we'll beat 'em. We've got 'em beat," Bud would reply.

Hannah, to check herself against the sin of overconfidence, would break in with, "Now, don't you be too sure; there ain't been no man so good that there wasn't somebody bettah." But all the while her face and manner betrayed her words. "Now, let your brother be, Little Sista."

The great day came. A crowd of people packed the great baseball grounds to overflowing. It was an eager, banner-waving, shouting crowd. It was strictly divided, and so the people separated themselves into sections by the colors of the flags they carried and the ribbons they wore. Side yelled at side, and party teased party. The blue and white of Company A flaunted boldly on the breeze beside the very seats over which the crimson and gray of B were flying, and they in their turn nodded defiance over the imaginary barrier between themselves and C's black and yellow.

The band thundered out Sousa's "High School Cadet's March." School officials, judges, reporters, and some with less purpose hurried about discussing and conferring. All was noise, hurry, joy, and confusion.

In the midst of it all, with blue and white rosettes pinned on their chests, sat two spectators, tense and silent. It seemed too much to Hannah and Little Sister to laugh and shout. They knew Bud was off somewhere with Company A preparing, and so the whole program felt more like a religious ceremony to them.

CHAPTER THREE

⚜

Company A

Hannah's face glowed with hope, and Little Sister sat very still and held her mother's hand except when, amid a burst of cheers, Company A swept into the parade ground at a quick step. Then, she sprang up, crying shrilly, "There's Bud! There's Bud! I see him!" and then melted back in her seat, slightly embarrassed. The mother's eyes danced as soon as the sister's had singled out their dear one from the midst of the blue-coated boys. It was hard for her to keep from following her little daughter's example.

Company A came swinging down the field toward the judges in a manner that called for more enthusiastic huzzahs that lifted many in the crowd to their feet. They were, indeed, a set of fine-looking young fellows, brisk, straight, and soldierly in bearing. Their captain was proud of them, and his very step showed it. He was like a skilled operator pressing the key of some great mechanism, and at his command, they moved like clockwork. Seen from the side, it was as though they were all bound together by inflexible iron bars, and as the end man moved, all must move with him.

The crowd was full of cries of praise and admiration, but a tense quiet came over them as Company A came

from columns of four into a line for volley firing. This was a real test. It meant not only grace and precision of movement, singleness of attention and steadiness, but quickness tempered by self-control. At the command, the volley rang forth like a single shot. This was again the signal for wild cheering, and the blue and white streamers kissed the sunlight swiftly and impulsively. Hannah and Little Sister drew closer together and held hands.

The A supporters, however, were considerably cooled when the Company's next volley began, badly scattering, with one shot entirely apart and before the rest. Bud's mother did not entirely understand the sudden quieting of the crowd; she felt vaguely that all was not as it should be, and the chill of fear laid hold upon her heart.

What if Bud's company (it was always "Bud's company" to them) should lose? But of course, that couldn't be. Bud himself had said they would win. Suppose, though, they didn't; and with these thoughts, they were miserable until the cheering again told them that the company had redeemed itself.

Someone behind Hannah said, "They are doing splendidly. They'll win; they'll win yet, in spite of the second volley."

Company A was back in columns of four. They executed the right oblique in double time and halted amid cheers; then formed left front into line without halting. The next movement was one looked forward to with much anxiety, on account of its difficulty. The order was marching by fours to fix or unfix bayonets. They were going at a quick step, but the boys' hands were steady—hope was bright in their hearts. They were doing it rapidly and freely, when suddenly from the ranks there was the bright gleam of steel lower down than it should have been.

A gasp broke.

Those in blue and white dropped sadly, while a few who wore other colors attempted to jeer.

Someone had dropped his bayonet.

But with muscles unquivering, without a turned head, the company moved on as if nothing had happened. One of the judges, an army officer, stepped into the wake of the boys and picked up the fallen steel.

CHAPTER FOUR

⚔

Shock and Disbelief

No two eyes had seen half so quickly as Hannah's and Little Sister's who the blunderer was. In the whole drill, there had been but one figure for them, and that was Bud. It was he who had dropped his bayonet. Nervous with the desire to please them, perhaps with a bit too much of thought of them watching with hearts in their eyes, he had fumbled and lost all he was striving for. His head went round and round. All seemed black before him.

He executed the movements in a dazed way. The applause, generous and sympathetic, as his company left the parade ground, came to him from far off. Like a wounded animal, he crept away from his comrades, not because their reproaches stung him, for he did not hear them, but because he wanted to think what his mother and Little Sister would say. His misery was nothing to that of the two who sat up there amid the ranks of the blue and white, holding each other's hands with a pained grip.

To Bud, all the rest of the contest was a horrid nightmare; he hardly knew when the three companies were marched back to receive the judges' decision. The applause that greeted Company B when the blue ribbons were pinned on the members' coats meant nothing to his ears. He had disgraced

himself and his company. What would his mother and little sister say?

To Hannah and Little Sister, as to Bud, the rest of the drill was a misery. The one interest they had in it failed, and not even the dropping of a gun by one of Company E's members when on the march could raise their spirits. The little girl tried to be brave, but when it was all over, she was glad to hurry out before the crowd got started and to hasten away home. Once she was there, her tears flowed freely; she hid her face in her mother's dress and sobbed as if her heart would break.

"Don't cry, baby! Don't cry. This ain't the last time there's gonna be a drill. Bud will have another chance, and then he'll show 'em somethin'."

But this comfort was nothing to Little Sister. It was so terrible to her, this failure of Bud's. She couldn't blame him or anyone else, and she had not yet learned to lay all such misfortunes at the door of fate. What was the thought of another day, another chance?

CHAPTER FIVE

Family Discussion

Her mother finally set about making supper, while Little Sister drooped disconsolately in her own little splint-bottom chair. She sat there weeping silently until she heard the sound of Bud's step, then sprang up and ran away to hide. She didn't dare face him with tears in her eyes. Bud came in without a word and sat down in the dark front room.

"That you, Bud?" asked his mother.

"Yes'm."

"Bettah come now, supper's pretty nigh ready."

"I don't want no supper."

"You bettah come on, Bud. I reckon you mighty tired."

He did not reply, but just then, a pair of thin arms were put around his neck and a soft cheek was placed close to his own.

"Come on, Buddie," whispered Little Sister. "Mama an' me know you didn't mean to do it, an' we don't care."

Bud threw his arms around his little sister and held her tightly.

"It's only you an' Ma I care about," he said, "though I am sorry I spoiled the company's drill. They say B would have won anyway on account of our bad firing, but I did want you and Ma to be proud."

"We is proud," she whispered. "We

is almos' prouder than if you had won."

And pretty soon, she led him by the hand to supper. Hannah did all she could to cheer the boy and to encourage him to hope for next year, but he had little to say in reply and went to bed early.

In the morning, though it neared school time, Bud lingered around and seemed in no disposition to get ready to go.

"Bettah get ready for school," said Hannah cheerily.

"I don't believe I want to go anymore," Bud replied.

"Not go anymore? Why, ain't you ashamed to talk that way! Of course you goin' to school."

"I'm ashamed to show my face to the boys."

"What you say about the boys? The boys ain't goin' to give you an education when you need it."

"Oh, I don't want to go, Ma; you don't know how I feel."

"I'm kinda sorry I let you go into that company," said Hannah musingly, "'cause it was the teachin' I wanted you to get, not the prancin' and steppin'; but I did think it would make more of a man of you, and it ain't. Your pappy was a poor man, hard workin', and he wasn't high-class neither. But from the time I first see him to the day of his death, I nevah seen him back down because he was afraid of anything." And with that, Hannah turned to her work.

Little Sister went up and slipped her hand in his. "You ain't gonna back down, is you, Buddie?" she said.

"No," said Bud stoutly, as he braced his shoulders. "I'm going."

But no persuasion could make him wear his uniform.

CHAPTER SIX

❈

Redemption

Some boys were a little cold to him. Some were brutal. But most of them recognized the fact that what had happened to Bud Harris might have happened to any one of them. Besides, since the percentage had been shown, it was found that B had outpointed them in many ways, and so their loss was not due to the one grave error.

Bud's heart sank when he dropped into his seat in the Assembly Hall to find one of the blue-coated officers who had acted as judge the day before on the platform. After the opening exercises were over, he was called upon to address the school. He spoke readily and pleasantly, laying special stress upon the value of discipline.

Toward the end of his address,

he said, "I suppose Company A is heaping accusations upon the head of the young man who dropped his bayonet yesterday." Bud could have died. "It was most regrettable," the officer continued, "but to me the most significant thing at the drill was the conduct of that cadet afterward. I saw the whole proceeding. I saw that he did not pause for an instant, that he did not even turn his head. It appeared to me as one of the finest bits of self-control I had ever seen in any youth. Had he forgotten himself for a moment and stopped, however quickly, to secure the weapon, the next line would have been interfered with and your whole movement thrown into confusion." There were a half hundred eyes glancing at Bud, and the light began to dawn in his face. "This boy has shown what discipline means, and I for one want to shake hands with him, if he is here."

When he had concluded, the

principal called Bud forward, and the boys, even his critics, cheered as the officer took his hand.

"Why are you not in uniform, sir?" he asked.

"I was ashamed to wear it after yesterday," was the reply.

"Don't be ashamed to wear your uniform," the officer said to him. Bud could have fallen on his knees and thanked him.

There were no more jeers from his comrades, and when he related it all at home that evening, there were two more happy hearts in that south Washington cottage.

"I told you we was more prouder dan if you'd won," said Little Sister.

"And what did I tell you about backin' out?" asked his mother.

Bud was too happy and too busy to answer. He was brushing his uniform.

About Us

The Author

Paul Laurence Dunbar became a poet in the late 1800s. He was one of the first internationally recognized African American poets. Both of his parents were formerly enslaved people. Despite being a successful high school student, college was not an option. He became an elevator operator and paid to print his first volume of poems. In some of his work, he featured the language of the African American South, using the language of his community.

The Illustrator

Luigi Savino grew up doodling on notepads in the back of his family's restaurant. While attending school, he developed his artistic skill, his love for hip-hop music, and a bagel habit. He started his career designing concert posters and logos among other things. He now lives in Oakland, California, with his partner, Ruby, and their dog.